W9-ACI-385

STUTSMAN COUNTY LIBRARY
BOOKMOBILE
Books for Everyone

JUST ME AND MY COUSIN

BY GINA AND MERCER MAYER

For Laura Gilliam

A GOLDEN BOOK • NEW YORK
Western Publishing Company, Inc. Racine, Wisconsin 53404

 Library of Congress Catalog Card Number: 92-71683. ISBN: 0-307-12688-9/ISBN: 0-307-62688-1 (lib. bdg.)
MCMXCII

We went to visit my cousin and
my aunt and uncle. I brought my bike
and some of my favorite toys.

I showed my bike to my cousin.
He said, "Mine is faster." So we had a race.
My cousin won.

He showed me his tree house.
He dared me to climb up, so I did.

Then my cousin pushed the ladder away. I started to cry. My cousin tried to put the ladder back, but it was too heavy. My uncle had to come and help.

I showed my Super Critter doll to my cousin.
"Let's see how far Super Critter can fly," he said.
He threw my doll out the window.

I was so mad. But then he helped me
find Super Critter. And he brushed him off.

We built a robot with my uncle's tools.
Then my uncle came and told us
we weren't supposed to use his tools.
I didn't know that.

My cousin and I had to put everything away.
We didn't even get to finish our robot.

We played checkers.
First my cousin was winning.
Then I was winning.

My cousin knocked
the checkerboard over.
Nobody won.

Later we had a pillow fight. My cousin hit me real hard. I tried to hit him back real hard. I missed and hit the lamp real hard instead.

It fell on the floor and broke.

We played hide-and-seek.
I hid first.

Then my cousin hid.
I couldn't find him.

Then a monster jumped out
from behind the door.
It chased me downstairs.

My aunt caught the monster.
It was just my cousin.

“Let’s play some more,” my cousin said.
But I didn’t want to play with him.
I was too mad.

Finally Mom said, “It’s time to go home.”
I was glad. I got my jacket on.

Then my cousin came downstairs and handed me a piece of paper. It said, "I'm sorry."

And he looked like he was sorry.

Maybe my cousin isn't so bad after all.